SKYLARK CHOOSE YOUR OWN ADVENTURE® • 50

"I DON'T LIKE CHOOSE YOUR OWN ADVENTURE® BOOKS. I *LOVE* THEM!" says Jessica Gordon, age ten. And now, kids between the ages of six and nine can choose their own adventures too. Here's what kids have to say about the Skylark Choose Your Own Adventure® books.

"These are my favorite books because you can pick whatever choice you want—and the story is all about you."

—**Katy Alson,** *age 8*

"I love finding out how my story will end."

—**Joss Williams,** *age 9*

"I like all the illustrations!"

—**Savitri Brightfield,** *age 7*

"A six-year-old friend and I have lots of fun making the decisions together."

—**Peggy Marcus** *(adult)*

Bantam Skylark Books in the Choose Your Own Adventure® series
Ask your bookseller for the books you have missed

#2 THE HAUNTED HOUSE
#6 THE GREEN SLIME
#37 HAUNTED HALLOWEEN PARTY
#40 THE GREAT EASTER BUNNY ADVENTURE
#46 A DAY WITH THE DINOSAURS
#47 SPOOKY THANKSGIVING
#48 YOU ARE INVISIBLE
#49 RACE OF THE YEAR
#50 STRANDED!
#51 YOU CAN MAKE A DIFFERENCE:
THE STORY OF MARTIN LUTHER KING, JR.
#52 THE ENCHANTED ATTIC

STRANDED!

SARA COMPTON

ILLUSTRATED BY LESLIE MORRILL

An Edward Packard Book

A BANTAM SKYLARK BOOK®
NEW YORK · TORONTO · LONDON · SYDNEY · AUCKLAND

RL 2, 007-009

STRANDED!
A Bantam Skylark Book / November 1989

CHOOSE YOUR OWN ADVENTURE® is a registered trademark of Bantam Books, a division of Bantam Doubleday Dell Publishing Group, Inc.
Registered in U.S. Patent and Trademark Office and elsewhere.

Original conception of Edward Packard

Skylark Books is a registered trademark of Bantam Books, a division of Bantam Doubleday Dell Publishing Group, Inc.
Registered in U.S. Patent and Trademark Office and elsewhere.

Cover art by Bill Schmidt
Interior illustrations by Leslie Morrill

ISBN 0-553-15762-0

Published simultaneously in the United States and Canada

Bantam Books are published by Bantam Books, a division of Bantam Doubleday Dell Publishing Group, Inc. Its trademark, consisting of the words "Bantam Books" and the portrayal of a rooster, is Registered in U.S. Patent and Trademark Office and in other countries. Marca Registrada. Bantam Books, 666 Fifth Avenue, New York, New York 10103.

PRINTED IN THE UNITED STATES OF AMERICA

OPM 0 9 8 7 6 5 4

STRANDED!

READ THIS FIRST!!!

Most books are about other people.

This book is about you! What happens to you while you are stranded depends on the choices you make.

Do not read this book from the first page through to the last. Instead, start on page one and read until you come to your first choice. Then decide what you want to do, turn to the page shown, and see what happens.

When you come to the end of a story, go back and start again. Every choice leads to a new adventure.

Are you ready to be rescued from the desert island you have been stranded on? Then turn to page one—and good luck!

You are on a big luxury liner, crossing the Pacific Ocean with your aunt Rose and cousin Lydia. It had sounded like fun when they invited you to join them on their vacation, but after three days at sea you almost wish you were home again.

The problem is Lydia—*bossy* Lydia. She's only eight months older than you are, but she's always ready to tell you what to do. You never ask her, but still she tells you what to order for breakfast, which shirt to put on, and even when to go to bed!

But now you've finally managed to ditch Lydia. You challenged her to a game of hide and seek. The last you saw of her, she was running toward some big crates, looking for a place to hide.

You smile as you think of Lydia, crouched behind a crate, waiting to be found. You look out over the turquoise water. The ocean is very calm, smooth as glass.

You look at the horizon. A swell of water moves toward you. Then you gasp as it turns into a gigantic wall of water!

Turn to page 6.

You pull your tired body onto the crate and stretch out in the warm sun. Soon you're fast asleep, rocked by the gentle motion of the waves.

A few hours later you're jolted awake as the crate enters shallow water. Before you is a sandy beach and a lush tropical forest.

You can't wait to feel dry land under your feet! You jump down into the surf, but without your weight to hold the crate down, it starts to float away.

Maybe you should try to haul it toward shore. There might be something useful inside. But the thought of staying anywhere near water so soon after almost drowning makes you hesitate.

If you try to haul the crate to shore with you, turn to page 22.

If you decide to forget about the crate, turn to page 10.

You make a run for the tree. The gorilla is faster than you are, but he has more distance to cover. Still, you can feel his breath as you grab a branch and scramble up into the tree.

Once you're safe, you look down from your perch above the gorilla. You can't help gloating about the way you pulled off your escape.

"The trouble with you gorillas," you yell down, "is you can't climb trees!"

They don't have to, you soon learn, as you feel the tree whipping violently back and forth. If a gorilla wants something he can't reach in a tree, all he has to do is shake it out!

Now you are left wondering if you can hang on longer than he can shake. Only time will tell.

The End

You watch in horror as the huge wave draws closer. It towers over the luxury liner, blotting out the sun, and then . . . CRASH!!

The force of the water sweeps you overboard, into the violent sea. Another wave throws you up into the air. You just manage one quick breath before you're plunged deep into the water once again.

When you come to the surface, you see the ship sailing on through the sea. No one seems to know you've been swept overboard!

Turn to page 16.

"We've already radioed ahead. Your aunt Rose knows you're coming home," the captain tells you once you're on board the freighter. "Of all the people who were swept overboard, you and Lydia are the last to be found."

As the freighter picks up speed, you wave to Utu until he's just a tiny dot on the shore.

You're heading for home, now, but somehow, it feels like you're *leaving* home. You know you'll miss your friends, and the island paradise you grew to love. *If only you could leave your cousin Lydia behind, instead of Utu,* you think.

The End

Whatever's in that crate is probably all wet and disgusting by now, you think as you watch a big wave carry it away.

As you run toward land, you notice steep, rocky cliffs rising from the beach along the shoreline. If you could climb to the top, you might be able to see the whole island—and spot a likely place to find food.

But when you reach the sand you see a path leading through the jungle. There's a good chance that it will lead you to something to eat or drink, but you'll have to be careful. You could run into whoever—or *whatever*—made the path.

If you decide to follow the path,
turn to page 39.

If you try to climb the cliff,
turn to page 25.

Quickly you sort through the jumbled contents of Lydia's knapsack: lip gloss, hot comb, Barbie doll, but no mirror. Then, in desperation, you open Barbie's purse, and there it is!

Lydia continues shouting toward the super tanker as you calmly aim the tiny mirror toward the sun. A beam of light bounces off the mirror's surface as you flash the international code of distress.

The mirror is small, but it works! Slowly the boat turns and heads straight toward you.

"I saved us!" screams Lydia. She looks at you scornfully. "And all *you* did was stand there!"

Turn to page 33.

You smile at the gorilla, hoping to make friends with him. The gorilla roars again—but not as loudly as before.

You slowly sink to the ground and sit quietly as several more gorillas appear. One of them is eating a juicy piece of fruit. "Mmmmm, that looks good," you say.

The gorillas seem a bit more relaxed, and so are you. "Nice looking kid," you say to a big gorilla carrying a baby.

You talk until the gorillas stop listening. They seem to be ignoring you, so cautiously—*very* cautiously—you pick up a piece of fruit.

It's delicious! And so are all the other fruits, nuts, and vegetables these new friends teach you to eat.

It isn't long before it's *your* jungle, too. You still want to go home, but for now, at least, you are safe.

The End

Lydia may be right, you think. "It might be dangerous," you say, looking uneasily at the dense jungle. "But what are we going to do for food and water?"

Lydia points to some large seashells lying on the beach. "We can collect rainwater," she says. Then she dumps the contents of her purse out on the sand. "And I have enough candy bars to last at least a month!"

"I don't know, Lydia," you say. "It might be safer to stay right here. But I don't think we can live on candy bars. There may be fruit and nuts in the jungle."

If you decide to stay where you are and wait to be rescued, turn to page 45.

If you persuade Lydia to explore the island with you, turn to page 36.

You try to keep your head above water, but you're tossed about like a toy. Then, just when you think you can't last another minute, the churning stops. With your last bit of strength, you swim for your only hope of survival—a big wooden crate floating in the water near you.

Turn to page 3.

As you near the top of the hill, you're relieved to see blue sky and sunshine up ahead. In fact, you're smiling as you round the last curve and enter a clearing.

But the smile suddenly fades from your face and you stop dead in your tracks. Ahead on the path, not ten feet away, is a gorilla. And he's not smiling either!

Turn to page 27.

"I'll handle this!" says Lydia as you land on the beach. "Take me to the nearest telephone!" she says grandly.

The natives stare blankly at you and Lydia. Then you have an idea. You pantomime paddling out to a big ship. Then, despite Lydia's protests, you give them the last of her candy bars.

Before long the natives understand what you mean, and they paddle you and Lydia out to a ship. You're rescued!

The End

"Here goes!" you say as you grab the rocky ledge and push off into the air.

Straining with all your might, you manage to heave yourself up over the edge. You sit, panting, waiting for your body to stop shaking from the hard work. Then you climb the rest of the way to the top.

It was worth the climb, you think. What a view! You can see a waterfall, some fruit trees—and miles and miles of empty sea.

You head for the waterfall, eating bananas along the way.

Turn to page 34.

You might be able to use whatever's inside the crate, you decide. You push it toward the shore, then shove it through the wet sand until it won't go any farther. You're wondering how to get the top off when it springs wide open. A dazed but familiar face appears.

"Oh, no," you gasp. "It's you!"

"Well, don't just stand there bug-eyed," your cousin Lydia snaps. "Get me out of here!" You pull her out of the crate. She shakes water from her ears and pulls a handkerchief from her knapsack to dry herself.

"Come on," you say. "Let's look around!"

"We're not going into that jungle," Lydia says icily. "We're staying right here on this beach until we're rescued. Jungles are full of horrid animals, huge bugs, and poisonous plants."

They can't be any worse than bossy cousins, you think to yourself.

Turn to page 14.

You walk to the base of what looks like a sixty-foot cliff. You take a deep breath and begin inching your way up. It's not easy to find footholds on the smooth rock, and you don't dare look down!

You're almost to the top when you feel the rocks under your feet start to give way. There's a solid-looking ledge just over your head. You're not sure you have enough strength left to pull yourself up onto it. But if you can get there, the rest of the climb should be easy.

It might be safer to slide down and look for another way to the top. But what if the crumbling rocks turn into an avalanche?

If you try to pull yourself up on the ledge, turn to page 21.

If you decide to slide down and look for another route to the top, turn to page 41.

The gorilla pounds on his chest and roars. You're shaking with fear, but you tell yourself not to panic as you try to think what to do.

If you try to scare the gorilla and roar back,
turn to page 29.

If you try to make friends with the gorilla,
turn to page 12.

I'm not letting any gorilla tell me what to do, you think. You take a deep breath, pound your chest, and bellow as loud as you can, "AAAAAARRRRRRGGGGHHH!!!"

The gorilla leaps back a few feet. He seems surprised that a creature your size is so brave, and so *noisy.*

There's a tree about four feet away. Maybe you should try to make a run for it while he's confused. Then you could climb up out of his reach.

Or you could stand your ground. Think of the fun you'd have telling your friends back home how you outroared a gorilla!

If you decide to stand your ground, turn to page 50.

If you run for the tree, turn to page 4.

Lydia's shouts to attract the super tanker's attention grow more frantic as you swim out to the canoe. But by the time you paddle back to pick her up, the tanker has disappeared.

"If you'd helped with the yelling, we could have been rescued by now," she grumbles as she gets in.

You paddle across the water toward the island, but it's very difficult; you're not used to paddling canoes through ocean waters! You can see people gathering on the beach to meet you.

Turn to page 19.

"I've had enough adventure for one day," you say. "My head hurts, and I don't want to move."

The boy seems to understand. He pushes his canoe back into the water and paddles away. You watch until you can no longer see him.

Then you notice the dried fish and coconut milk he left for you. "I guess he was a friend after all," you say.

Turn to page 52.

It isn't until the ship's captain welcomes you aboard that Lydia learns what really happened.

"So what?" she sniffs. "I was the one who was smart enough to get stranded with a mirror."

The captain winks at you, and says to Lydia, "Getting stranded with your cousin was even smarter." Lydia stomps off in a huff as you and the captain share a good laugh.

The End

After a shower under the falls, you hike farther inland.

Over the next few days, you explore most of the island. You see a band of gorillas—but no human life. You find enough fruit and nuts to eat, and you make a tree house out of drift-wood.

Then one day you see an airplane. It's too far away to see you, but it gives you an idea.

For days you carry huge stones to a large clearing. There you arrange them to form a giant word, *help.*

Your plan works. A seaplane picks you up and soon you're back home with an amazing story to tell. It will be a long time before you eat another banana, though.

The End

HELP

"We can't live on Dr. Chewies for very long," you say. "We've got to find more food. I think we should explore the island."

"Okay, we'll walk down the beach," says Lydia, reluctantly.

As you walk, you find some berries to eat, and plenty of bananas. Then you round a curve in the beach and see another island on the horizon. You hear the sound of drumbeats from that direction, and voices chanting.

You notice a small dugout canoe floating just offshore. "Let's swim out and grab it," you say eagerly. "We can use it to get to the island. There must be a settlement over there!"

Turn to page 46.

Cautiously, you follow the path and enter the jungle. The branches overhead are so thick that it gets darker and darker with each step. Insects swarm around you, biting at your skin. You hope they're not poisonous, but there's nothing you can do about it now.

As you follow the twisting path you try not to think about what you might run into around the next curve. You walk slowly, watching where you step, hoping to avoid any deadly snakes that might be waiting for you.

Your heart is pounding as you carefully pick your way through thorny vines as thick as your arm. Then you notice the path is leading you up a steep hill.

Turn to page 17.

Impatient to find a safer route to the top, you slide down the rocky slope as fast as you can. But the loose rocks slide right along with you. The sandy beach is only six feet below you when a rock hits the back of your head. Everything goes black.

When you come to, you're looking up into the brown eyes of a boy about your age.

"*O pao!*" he says, urgently pointing to a canoe on the beach. "*Unga woh!*"

You don't know if you're about to make a friend or an enemy, but you do know you've never had such a headache.

If you go with the boy, turn to page 48.

If you stay where you are, turn to page 31.

Your rescuers turn out to be the gentlest, kindest people you've ever met. They share their food and shelter, and soon you can understand most of the things they say.

One day you're gathering food with your new friend, Utu. "There are lots of bananas over there," you say, pointing to the island you washed up on.

"That island belongs to the gorillas," he tells you. "They don't take our food, and we don't take theirs."

A week later, a big freighter appears off on the horizon. The villagers build a huge bonfire, and soon a rescue party arrives to pick you up.

Turn to page 9.

It's safer to stay where you are, you decide. The candy bars Lydia has only last two days, but that's okay. After forty-three Dr. Chewies, you don't feel like eating anything else anyway. And the last thing you want to do is go into the jungle to look for food.

Lydia isn't the least bit worried. "So what if we're out of candy bars," she says. "I know just what to do next!"

"What's that?" you ask.

"Burn the wrappers!" she replies. "Someone's bound to see the fire and come save us."

You figure the chances are slim, but you don't tell Lydia. She won't listen to you anyway. And besides, the way it looks, the two of you may be together for a long time. The island is now your new home.

The End

But just then Lydia starts shouting and frantically jumping up and down. She's looking at something way off on the horizon.

It's a super tanker! And she's trying to attract its attention.

"It's much too far away to see us," you tell Lydia, hopelessly. "If only we had a mirror, we could try to flash a signal!"

Then your eye falls on Lydia's knapsack. You don't have a mirror, but maybe Lydia does.

But the canoe is drifting farther away. If you don't grab it now, it'll be too late!

If you look through Lydia's knapsack for a mirror, turn to page 11.

If you swim for the canoe before it drifts away, turn to page 30.

The boy smiles and gives you some coconut milk and dried fish. Together you push off the canoe and soon you've crossed a broad channel, heading for a tiny settlement.

The boy's whole village turns out to meet you. Among the strange faces you spot one that is all too familiar.

"Lydia!" you exclaim. "How did *you* get here?"

"I washed up on shore in that crate," she says, pointing to the big wooden crate that saved your life when you were washed overboard.

Turn to page 42.

50 "You think you're hot stuff," you say tauntingly, standing your ground. "Well get a load of this!" You pound your chest and let out another earsplitting roar.

The gorilla stares at you. He's given you fair warning. Now he'll have to do the only other thing he knows to defend against an enemy.

The charge is so fast, you just have time to remember a sign you once read at a zoo:

DO NOT TEASE THE ANIMALS

Too bad you didn't think of it sooner.

The End

DO NOT TEASE THE ANIMALS

52 The boy is the last human you see for a long time. Years later a passing ship spots you and sends a lifeboat to pick you up.

Back home again, you're asked to appear on all the TV talk shows. But they'll have to wait. It's been so long, you've forgotten how to speak!

The End

ABOUT THE AUTHOR

Sara Compton has created hundreds of songs and sketches for *Sesame Street* and other television shows, and is the recipient of five Emmys. She is also the inventor of a board game, Letter Loops.

ABOUT THE ILLUSTRATOR

Leslie Morrill is a designer and illustrator whose work has won him numerous awards. He has illustrated over thirty books for children, including the Bantam Classic edition of *The Wind in the Willows*. Mr. Morrill has illustrated *Danger Zones, The First Olympics, Inca Gold, Stock Car Champion, Alien, Go Home, Grave Robbers, The Treasure of the Onyx Dragon, Fight for Freedom, Smoke Jumper, Behind the Wheel, Silver Wings*, and *Showdown* in the Choose Your Own Adventure® series.